3791

D1312563

Yeah.

HOW TO TRAIN YOUR HUMAN (FOR DOGS)
by
Marcello Von Cauliflower
Bonaparte Jackson

$1.49

TENNESSEE
NASHVILLE
MEMPHIS
KNOXVILLE
TRI-CITIES
CHATTANOOGA

248. Temple of the Sibyl. Early 1st century

EVERYTHING is MINE

ANDREA D'AQUINO

My name is Marcello Von Cauliflower Bonaparte Jackson.

My friends just call me Marcello.

As you can probably tell, I'm kind, clever and very loyal.

Oh, and in case you haven't heard, everything is mine.

This slipper, for example.

We are both furry and cute.
I suspect we can have some fun together.

Plus, my mum still has one of them.
Why would anyone need two?

This slipper is mine.

Bold move, dude.

Do you see anyone's
name on this pork chop?
Me neither.

I left the carrots for Leo.

This must be **mine**.

Do you have any documentation
for that acorn, Squirrel?

I didn't think so.

Let's agree to call it mine,
shall we?

I also claim ownership of this tree.
Now I'll have all the sticks that
I could ever chew, all for myself.

Don't these dogs know that this is my park
and therefore they must follow my rules?

Most are very disrespectful of my authority.
It doesn't matter. This park is still mine.

One day I plan to write a book about them,
so they know how carefully I'm watching
their every move.

Whatever.

Ha ha,
you have to
go home now.

What do you mean that it's time
to put on my leash and go home?

All of **my** ideas are always
so much better than yours!

I found a good way
to stay busy at home.
These letters
looked so boring.

I got very creative.
I tore them up
and made them into
a work of art that is

100% mine.

Not your
best work,
sir.

I think it's time that we all come to grips with the reality that this home and this entire building is **mine.**

Can someone please explain to me what is happening?

And then, logically speaking, this whole city is mine.

If I could negotiate with the world's powers, they would likely agree that the entire country, continent and surrounding oceans are rightfully mine.

I claim them for myself under international law, treaty #49, hereby known as the Marcello Von Cauliflower Bonaparte Jackson Treaty. 🐾

🐾 *This is a footnote, or a paw note, which means that I may add more places to my empire, such as the rest of the whole wide world, for example.*

Furthermore, I can see a
whole universe out there!

That means that there are
approximately 100,000,000,000
solar systems that I named after myself.

Which is just another way
to say that they are mine.

This is not what
I expected to be
doing today.

To avoid any further questions,
I made a list of all the stuff that belongs to me.

I consider this contract legally binding,
as my lawyer, a well-known bulldog, can confirm.

This is getting kind
of weird, right?

Rrruff.

An INCOMPLETE LIST
• of •
Marcello's Property

Yeah.

3791

Willendorf, *see* "Ve
William II, king of S
William of Sens, 393
William the Conqueror

$1.49

HOW TO
TRAIN YOUR
HUMAN
(FOR DOGS)
by
Marcello Von Cauliflower
Bonaparte Jackson

TENNESSEE
NASHVILLE   KNOXVILLE   TRI-CITIES
MEMPHIS   CHATTANOOGA

248. Temple of the Sibyl. Early 1st century

Lastly, the most prized of
my worldly possessions,

the crown jewel of my collection:

this homework
is mine!

"STOP!", Leo shouts.
"No way!
I worked hard on that.

That is
not yours."

G_{rrrrrrrrrrr}rrr

"Hold on, Marcello. I have an idea."

"Swap?"

Liver flavour?
Leo, we have a deal.

Maybe I don't really need *everything*.

I think all I really need is my friendship with Leo.

Our friendship is one of the most important things I have.

But can I share one more thought with you?

There are A LOT of things that are still mine!

Marcello would like to thank some of his best friends:
Oscar, Olive, Bubu, Chaplin, Chula, Roxie, Zeus, Mia, Guinness, Oscar (another one), Henri,
Pablo, Penelope, Edgar, Otie, Clint, Dobie, Duc d'Argent, Puck, Zach, Millie, Midas, Titus,
Arnold, Lola, Sandy, Linus, Pearl, Penny, Rudy, Garcia, Coco and so many others.

Marcello was a real dog with
a big personality, and Leo was his best friend.
He was a brown and white schnauzer
who liked to take things.
He also had a hot dog toy.

First published 2020 by order of the Tate Trustees
by Tate Publishing, a division of Tate Enterprises Ltd,
Millbank, London SW1P 4RG
www.tate.org.uk/publishing

Text and illustrations © Andrea D'Aquino 2020
Published by arrangement with Debbie Bibo Agency

A catalogue record for this book is available from the British Library

ISBN 978 1 84976 692 0

Distributed in the United States and Canada by ABRAMS, New York
Library of Congress Control Number applied for

Colour reproduction by Evergreen Colour Management Ltd
Printed and bound in China by C&C Offset Printing Co., Ltd